I0647126

Royal Boil

Anna Marie Isgro

Illustrated by fx and color studio

ROYAL MEDIA
PUBLISHING

Royal Media and Publishing
P. O. Box 4321
Jeffersonville, IN 47131
502-802-5385
http://www.royalmediaandpublishing.com
royalmediapublishing@gmail.com

Cover Design By: Elite Designs

ISBN-13: 978-1-955501-07-1

Printed in the United States of America

Dedication

Dedicated to all the King's princesses and princes who have been molested and raped by jacks and have been or still awaiting to be avenged by the Ace, our loving and just Savior & Lord Jesus Christ.

Preface

Nationally, in the United States of America, way over half of both men and women have reported being sexual harassed and /or assaulted in their lifetime, according to the National Sexual Violence Resource Center website, www.nsvrc.org. Also according to the World Health Organization, 40 million children all over the world are abused each year, as documented by the International Center for Assault Prevention's website, www.internationalcap.org. And that's just the reported sexual abuse. What happens to all of the other precious people who never report their casualties, whether out of fear or pride, and never get treated or ministered to?

We are all born loving perfect little babies into our environments we are not responsible for, and then life goes on. If we become victims of circumstances and events, we endure and either suffer or seek help as a victim to somehow become a victor.

It is my prayer that this poem will help you articulate your feelings and cause you to be victorious in Christ Jesus' Peace as you seek God's ways that He spoke of.

He hits the queen, jack of clubs,
deceiving to be king.
He plans to party at pubs
not knowing her heart's sting.

The jack is in big trouble.

The queen hates all his ways.

The king's decree will double.

Jack's running out of days.

Jack of diamonds robs the queen
to take her jewels and cash;
Strips her, crown and robe, so lean
and takes her royal sash.

The queen screams but no one cares;
her grace and kindness scorned.
Naked beauty, now Jack dares,
to rape the queen till morn.

While jacks are still touching her,
the queen now hits and kicks
and pokes their eyes to endure
her cutting off their dicks.

The jack of spades thinks to kill
while on the ground he lies
where on the red, grassy hill
now curls with cries and sighs.

The queen rises in the wind,
her spirit to the king,
to tell her Love, "jacks have sinned
and you must use your ring.

King of hearts in grief is torn
to see his Love so bruised.
Takes his club, the king has sworn:
Spade jack of hearts his dues.

King of diamonds will avow
a vast reward to snatch
all the jacks, to make them bow.
The people helped him catch.

Ten of diamonds chased his jack
and ran with nine and eight.
Seven and six followed back
with five and four as bait.

"Jack is in the house, that fiend!"
said the ten to the king.
The folks screamed "Long live the Queen!"
All people start to sing.

The king now calls on the ace
above to judge the jacks,
for the verdict on the case
exposing all the facts.

With great love for his royals
and people in the deck,
Ace now questions the loyals
if jacks should lose their neck.

Jury shouts in one accord,
"Off with their heads today!"
Tears from the ace's eyes had poured
to save the jacks some way.

The ace thought and remembered
when he went below two
to save the race so numbered
and make them all brand new.

But now jacks have ruined peace
and justice must prevail.
So Ace rules the king and queen
to lock jacks up in jail.

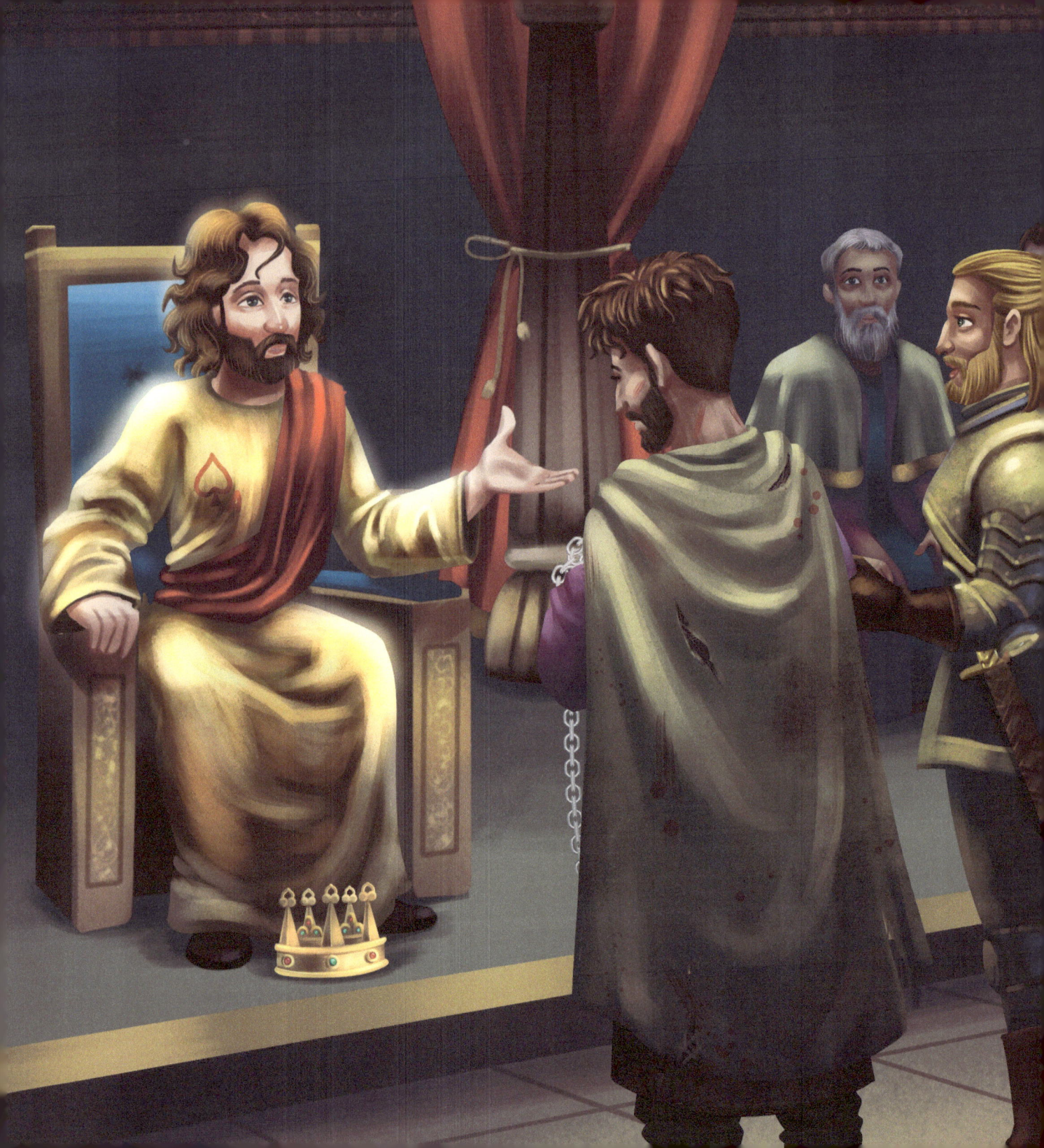

The numbers vexed in great wrath,
"Why not let the jacks die?"
Ace trumped saying, "Do the math:
jacks can't lose their heads twice."

The End

About the Author

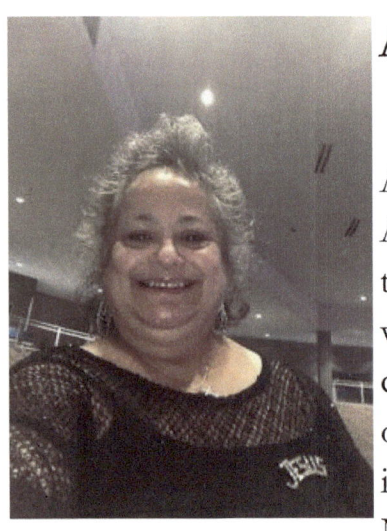

Anna Maria Isgro is the baby of five in a passionate Italian/Sicilian-American military family. Among many other spiritual gifts, skills and talents, she received her gift of being a singer/songwriter in 1983. In a vision of Christ Jesus showing her His hands on His lap, she was able to compose her first song, Work of the Artist, within a half hour at the age of 19. She has gone on to perfect her meter and songwriting style later in life while recording under a mentor and Nashville producer, (Hugh) Neal James and is still writing songs, poems, and stories.

She knows the childhood pains of divorce. And through growing up with her broken and hurting, divorced, single mother and brothers and sister, and all of them watching their mother cry, Anna Maria has learned to call on God as her Heavenly Father through Christ Jesus and prayed for God to bring Dad back home. Learning from her mother as an example of a hard worker who saved all her money from her second job to build her and her husband's Florida dream home, Anna Maria enlisted in the United States Air Force like her father and two elder brothers. After she graduated Basic Military Training School in January 1985, Mom and Dad decided to remarry each other after nine years of divorce, while visiting the old courthouse they were originally married in 1948 in Meridian, Mississippi. After seeing their daughter at her new military school, they were finally able to enjoy the Florida home together that they always dreamed of having.

Anna Maria was caretaker of her mother for twenty-five years, after honorably separating from the regular United States Air Force, until her mom's death at age 91 in 2016. Due to her rich background in the Word of God and traditional Italian customs, Anna Maria has stayed thirty years celibate, and counting, waiting for her soon-coming King Jesus Christ and right earthly king the Lord has prepared for her.

Anna Maria has run a global 24/7 ad-free radio broadcast called Worship Messiah Jesus at www.live365.com/station/a76673 since 2002, which airs vintage and contemporary intimate praise and worship music to our Lord and Savior Jesus Christ. In her spare time, she enjoys hobbies like painting her own Christmas cards, making her own Christmas gifts, and baking. She enjoys creating and giving homemade soaps, cosmetics, perfumes, and other fun stuff specific for each friend. She also enjoys her mother's vacation home in Florida and her two cats Leo and Lea Davida and her pet betta fish family that miraculously loves each other in the same, huge fish bowl in Christ's Love. Anna Maria has an Associates in Arts Degree from Pasco-Hernando State College in Florida and attends Life Christian University through distance learning. While at her Florida home, she helps her community at her local Church, Calvary Chapel Worship Center and volunteers her administrative skills for her Sheriff's Victim's Advocate.

Military life, as an Information Management Specialist in combat units and Airborne Warning and Control units, both stateside and overseas, opened the door to new life experiences and relationships, both bad and good. As a lady and a military veteran, and someone who left the Midwest Bible Belt dismayed, Anna Maria can empathize with anybody who has been traumatized, abused, misused and misunderstood. She learned that everything is a learning experience, and that we, as humans, are very frail. And we don't know how frail, and possibly immature, we really are until something extreme happens and our chemical make-up and what we're made from becomes evident. Not everybody can survive a divorce or a rape or assault the same way someone else can. And there is no judgment and condemnation. We are who we are. Some need medicine to cope. Some just give up because they can't afford medicine and don't have faith. And some have faith and still need medicine. And depending on the will of the Holy Ghost and the mixture of faith and love with forgiveness, some can reach the hem of Christ Jesus' garment and get a miracle and be instantly healed. Post-Traumatic Stress Disorder and mental illness are not always demonic.

Billy Graham said that sometimes it is very organic in nature due to psychological problems and depending on stressors and triggers. (Refer to Billy Graham's sermon from Mark chapter 5 at his Texas crusade entitled "Demon, Witches, and Wizards" discussing spiritual warfare. Go to: https://billygraham.org/audio/satan-witches-wizards-demons-and-jesus-2/). God searches our hearts.

Mental illness, although most examples in the Bible are demonic, it can be very human also. One of the causes of mental illness is fear, and St. Paul says God has not given us a spirit of fear but of love, power and a sound mind (2 Timothy 1:7). Adam and Eve in the Garden of Eden were in fear not only because they were naked, but also because they remembered God's warning of consequences of death. 1 John 4:18 NASB "There is no fear in love, but perfect love drives out fear, because fear involves punishment, and the one who fears is not perfected in love." They might not have died instantly as the serpent told them, but their spirit died instantly and could no longer commune with God nor the animals. (How else did they talk with a serpent?) But God! God sent His Anointed One, Christ Jesus, to give us new life by rebirthing our spirit and renew our souls and taking away our sins by His shed blood.

Anna Maria has kept her vow to The Lord and erected a cross at her Ohio home, to encourage homeless, hurting, street people who walk her streets day and night to know that God loves them and there is hope. She calls this Home at the Cross, which is under the umbrella of her Mission of Saint Mary at Jesus' Feet, which was birthed to encourage, educate and minister to the corporal and spiritual needs of hurting people, especially women, children and veterans. Your donations to Venmo @anna-isgro-1, or www.cash.app/$isgroanna, will not only support these ministries, but also will help stop human trafficking by shining the light of the preaching of the Gospel of Jesus Christ in power and true love of the Holy Ghost. A percentage of the proceeds from the sales of this book will also be offered to support these ministries, as well as her local church, Solid Rock Church, and other supportive churches in Hamilton, Ohio and the Tri-County area, such as God's Temple, Summit Church, Princeton Pike Church of God, City on a Hill (Cincinnati), and Heritage Fellowship (Florence, Kentucky).

To contact Anna Maria for booking speaking engagements or future concerts, or to schedule your concert or conference at her outdoors events for Home at the Cross, please email her at esushomefires@gmail.com or go to her website at www.annamaria.live.

You will also be able to buy her song, Royal Boil, as soon as it is produced, as well as her new debut album.

"It is finished!" Christ Jesus said on the Cross after shedding His sinless blood from becoming our sins and iniquities and diseases and sorrows (Isaiah 53, John 19:30). Christ took away all our sins.

Yes, if you commit the crime the Holy Spirit convicts you if you are a Christian and until you confess you are in a spiritual jail cell and only Christ can set you free when you are truly sorry and stop sinning against your neighbor, brother, and sister. And because Christ Jesus is Lord of Heaven and Earth as well, He will use His ordained peace officers as His servants to arrest you whether or not you are a Christian if you did the crime that you are not sorry for.

The Holy Spirit pleads with you to stop sinning and REPENT. 2 Chronicles 7:13:15 is often misread to pray for the nation including non-Christians; however, it was meant for God's people to turn from their wicked ways, not the world's wicked ways: "When I shut up heaven and there is no rain, or command the locusts to devour the land, or send pestilence among My people, if My people who are called by My name will humble themselves, and pray and seek My face, and turn from their wicked ways, then I will hear from heaven, and will forgive their sin and heal their land. Now My eyes will be open and My ears attentive to prayer made in this place."

The original eyewitness Jewish believing Apostles of Christ Jesus agreed together with St. Paul that Gentile believers in Christ needed to only follow four laws instead of the multitude of laws of Moses. These laws are recorded in the book of Acts written by St. Luke several times in Acts 15:20, 15:29, and 21:25. "As touching the Gentiles which believe, we have written and concluded that they observe no such thing, save only that they keep themselves from things offered to idols, and from blood, and from strangled, and from fornication." Fornication is all sexual immorality whether between married, as in adultery or single. (Bible also tells us to obey the laws of our government if it doesn't conflict with God's will. Romans 13:1 NKJV "Let every soul be subject to the governing authorities. For there is no authority except from God, and the authorities that exist are appointed by God.")

Hebrews 13:4 NKJV "Marriage is honorable among all, and the bed undefiled; but fornicators and adulterers God will judge."